Thank you to all my family and friends who have inspired, motivated and supported me through this process of making my dream of creating a children's book come true.

This book is dedicated to all the animals I have had in my life who gave me their unconditional love, and also to all my students past, present and future who fill my heart with immense joy. You are my purpose in life.

Please send children's drawings of Rufus & Olivia to Michele Walker. You may also contact her for book reading events at: rufusandolivia@gmail.com

Library of Congress Cataloging-in-Publication Data

Walker, Michele. Rufus & Olivia: A Tail of Acceptance p. cm.

ISBN 978-1-7371851-0-9

Summary: When Rufus comes into the home, Olivia must learn how to manage her new feelings. She learns from Rufus that we all have similarities and differences, and that is what makes us unique and special. They learn together what family is all about.

Quil.and.Ink thanks for bringing Rufus & Olivia's characters to life.

In memory of "Guy" who was the inspiration for Rufus.

Olivia is a cat who lives in a home with her two loving humans. She spends her days doing whatever she wants, and her nights cuddled up in bed next to her humans.

One day her humans come home saying, "Kitty! Here kitty kitty! Olivia, we have a surprise for you!"
Olivia pounced into the room excited for a surprise! *"Oh goodie!"* she thought. *"Cat treats? Maybe a new piece of furniture to climb? What did you bring me?"*

"Wait. What is that creature you are holding?!" Olivia exclaimed. "Did I approve of this? You did not ask my permission! Does this fur ball have fleas? You know dogs can't bathe themselves right?! Oh no! I think I'm getting a hair ball! Hack!"

"Look, Olivia!" said the woman. "Meet Rufus, your new brother!"

"He can't be my brother. We look different. I'm a cat. He's a dog. What were you thinking? I'm hungry. Where's my food?"

"Oh Olivia, he's cute and such a sweet dog. You two will grow to love each other", said the woman in a sweet voice.

"We shall see about that." Olivia said.

On the first day with the dog Olivia spent time observing him. *He appears to be not too bad, just scratches himself all the time. I told them he could have fleas. Do they not know fleas like cats too? Didn't I mention dogs can't bathe themselves? Oh Wow! Look now! He's chasing his tail.* "Boy that's a smart one they got!" Olivia announced.

The next day the man was teaching Rufus a trick
"Rufus can you sit?" The man said. Rufus laid down. "Come on Rufus sit. If you sit you can have a treat."
"Look! I'm sitting! Olivia exclaimed, "Where's my treat?"
"Ok Rufus darling can you lay down?" said the woman. Olivia laid down. "Look! Do you see I'm laying down?" Olivia announced proudly. Rufus watched Olivia and laid down just like her.

"Wait. What about me? No one cares about Olivia!" Olivia yelled "How about you teach him his tail is attached to his body. Look I have a tail too. Do you see me chasing it?" "Look can he do this yoga pose?" Olivia posed.

Olivia watches Rufus chase his tail around and around in a circle. "Rufus,
What do you plan to do when you catch your tail? You're making me dizzy!"

Rufus couldn't handle spinning in a circle anymore. He got dizzy and fell right over! Ker plop!

"Let me teach you something more relaxing Rufus. You need to connect with your body, and I don't mean by your mouth to your tail." "Okay. Watch and sit like me. Take a deep breath as I count to five. Breathe in 1, 2, 3, 4, 5 and out 1, 2, 3, 4, and 5. That's good! Let's try a yoga pose. Lift your leg Rufus like this, up boy! Can you do this too?" Olivia showed Rufus.

Rufus got distracted watching Olivia's example, and started scratching himself when trying to lift his leg in the air, and he fell right over! " Ay Chihuahua Rufus!"

The humans walked in. "Oh look you two are getting along!"

The woman said "We will be back in a little while. Olivia you are in charge. You need to help train Rufus. You two be good now."

Olivia came up with a plan. "Rufus do you want to play?" Rufus was excited Olivia asked him to play with her. He thought *she must be starting to like me now.* "Yes, I would like to play with you Olivia," Rufus said in an excited voice.

Olivia jumped up on the kitchen table. She saw a bowl of oranges. "Look Rufus Fetch!" And she knocked an orange on the floor. Rufus put it in his mouth and bit down, juice squirting everywhere! "Here how about another and another!" Olivia knocked them down one by one as Rufus tried to keep up squishing each orange in his mouth! Sticky juice squirted everywhere as more oranges rolled by!

Olivia then used her paw to pry open the cabinet door under the sink. "Rufus, there are treats in here." Rufus took in a big sniff with his nose and ended up with a banana peel stuck on his face. "How about getting some treats for you and I my smart pup?" Rufus knocks over the garbage can, and goes through everything! He tastes what he likes, leaving some fish smelling food for Olivia. " Ai yi yi silly boy!" Olivia said as she looked at all the scraps across the kitchen floor.

The humans came home to a fresh orange smell in the dining room, they walked across the sticky floor around the oranges like an obstacle course. The smell of oranges faded to a stinky old smell that came from the kitchen. "Rufus! What have you done?!" yelled the man.

"That is not good Rufus!" the man said. Rufus went and laid down on his bed. Olivia came walking by Rufus rubbing her fur by him teasing him.

Rufus said "Olivia why did you get me in trouble? I know I'm new in this family. I just want to be accepted and liked. Do you not like me?"
Olivia said "I'm trying Rufus. You are so different than me. I'm white. You are black. I'm a cat. You're a dog. Cats aren't supposed to like dogs. You beg for treats. Your scratching drives me crazy! You just are not smart like me"
Rufus just laid his head down, his eyes welling up with tears.

Rufus decided he would talk to Olivia to tell her how he feels. "You know Olivia, you really hurt my feelings today when you said those things to me. I wanted to tell you it really doesn't matter if we are black or white, or a cat or dog. We all have strengths. There are things you can do that I can't, and things I can do that you might not be able to do."

"We have similarities and differences and that's what makes us unique and special. Did you know Olivia that when I was born I had four siblings? One of my sister's was white. I had a brother and sister who were brown, and another brother who was black and white. My dad was a mix of white and brown. My mom was black and so beautiful. I am proud of my color. My color doesn't make me any different inside."

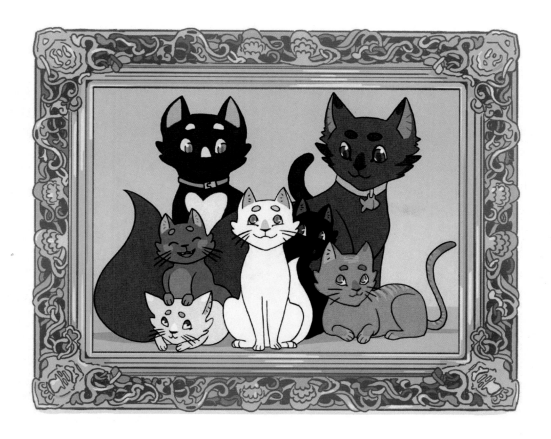

"Wow, you are right Rufus," said Olivia. I never thought about that. My family had different colors too. My siblings were white, grey and black. I even had a brother that was orange. We called him mama's little pumpkin. My mom was grey and my dad was black and white. We all looked different, but loved each other very much."

"Olivia, do you miss your animal family?" Rufus asked.

"Yes sometimes. They found homes with other families. That is what cats and dogs hope for, to be accepted and loved in a family. We both have humans that love us." Olivia said.

"Maybe we should call our humans mom and dad Olivia."

"I think that is a great idea Rufus. After all a mom and dad is love. We have a lot of love in our family."

"You are really smart Rufus, said Olivia sincerely. I misjudged you. I'm sorry for the words I said to you, and that I hurt your feelings. I wasn't very nice welcoming you to our family. I guess I was feeling like I wasn't getting mom and dad's attention anymore, and I became a little jealous of you. You are cute, fun, and do make me smile. You can help me understand what it's like to be a dog, and I can help you imagine what it's like to be a cat." Rufus said "We are alike in many ways and we are also different and that's okay."

"For example Olivia, we are both animals!"

Rufus, we both love naps! said Olivia

We both have four legs! said Rufus

Both our families come from many colors! said Olivia

"I like to watch you do yoga, Olivia, but I don't think it's for me" said Rufus

"I saw you fetch a toy Rufus. I can't do that, and that's okay" Olivia said

"Some of us are good at some things, and others are not so much. They might be better at something else," said Rufus.

"I like that you love to have fun Rufus. Be patient with me. I would really like to try to have fun like you sometime. I do not however enjoy walking on a leash, or getting into a bathtub or any form of water"

Rufus said, "That's okay Olivia. I do not enjoy going in a box. It kind of scares me a little bit, and I'm not very good at climbing like you. I am good at digging outside if you ever want me to keep one of your toys safe there."

"Thanks, Rufus. I do love you, little pup."

"Could I give you a hug Olivia?"

"Sure, Rufus. He pounced on Olivia with his paws around her and she wrapped her paws around him in a hug. They rolled around and then chased each other like a game of tag in the living room, narrowly missing the potted plants. Rufus then pulled on Olivia's tail with his mouth.

"Hey! now Rufus. Stop I don't like that!" Olivia said in a loud voice. Hey Rufus! I thought of another similarity we have. We both have tails! Even if you don't ever catch yours please don't pull mine ok

"Look Rufus! Mom and Dad grabbed their keys and are putting their shoes on. That's usually a clue they are going out somewhere."

"Follow me, Olivia!" Rufus went by mom and dad.

"Rufus, do you want to come for a ride?" said Dad

"Olivia, jump on my back! I've got you" Rufus cheered

"Don't be afraid Olivia. This will be fun! A new adventure for both of us" Rufus exclaimed. The window rolled down. Rufus stuck his head out the window the wind blowing his fur. His tongue out in pure happiness! He looked at Olivia, she put her head out too with a happy smile on her face.

"I'll keep my tongue in Rufus. I like to keep my polite kitty manners. But this is fun, like you Rufus. Thank you!" Olivia yelled over the car noise, and the sound of the wind blowing through the window.

"Here's to more adventures together Rufus!"

Questions to ask Children:

It's good to have conversations with your child/children or class about their feelings and the feelings of others. It's also important to have discussions about race with children. What is it about? It's ok to be different. We all are unique and have are own strengths that make us special. If we give children a foundation about racism, they will be more likely to speak up when they see injustices in their life. It's also important to know all families look different, and to practice acceptance of others that might be different than yours. Here are some questions you may choose from to start those conversations.

1. In the beginning of the story Olivia is expressing her feelings about Rufus coming into the home. Have you ever felt this way? What made you feel this way? What can you do to let your parent or teacher know how you are feeling?

2. How do you think Rufus feels when Olivia says unkind words to him? Have you ever felt this way by someone or have you heard someone speak unkind to another person? How did that make you feel? If you could have said something what would that be?

3. Rufus talks about the colors of his family he came from. "My color doesn't make me any different inside?" What does that mean to you? Should someone be treated differently because of the color they are born with? How can you be accepting of others that look different than you?
What can you do if you see someone treated poorly?

4. What does a family look like to you? Who can be a family?

5. Can you think of more similarities that Rufus and Olivia have or things they have in common? Can you understand the differences between them as a dog and a cat? What similarities do you have with any siblings or friends?

6. How do you feel when someone apologizes to you? How do you feel when someone gives you a compliment?

7. What strengths do you have that make you unique? What strengths does your siblings or friends have? What are some things you are good at? What are some things you would like to try?

8. Lastly which was your favorite page in the book and why?

Can you draw Rufus and olivia?

You can ask your parent for a piece of paper or use this page!
(Teachers you can give paper for your students to draw their representations.)

Drawings can be sent to the auther for possible posting at @Rufus_and_Olivia on Instagram or Rufus & Olivia Facebook page. You can email Michele Walker at rufusandolivia@gmail.com

Made in the USA
Middletown, DE
18 May 2021